MW01089669

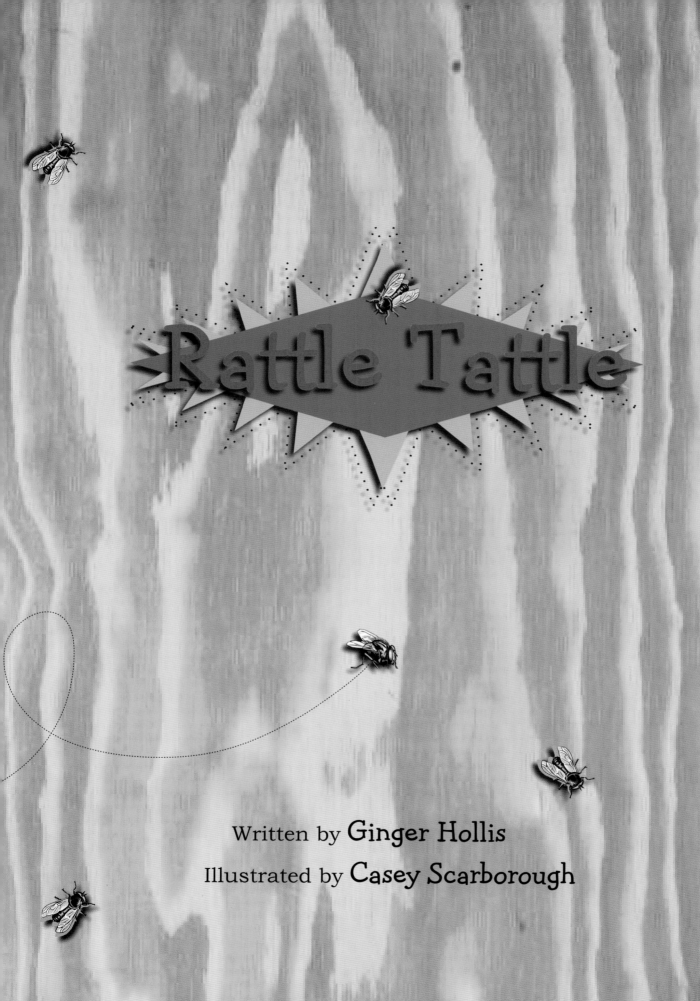

Rattle Tattle

Written by Ginger Hollis

Illustrated by Casey Scarborough

Rattle Tattle ©
copyright © 2007 JB Johnson Agency
Story by Ginger Hollis
Illustrations by Casey Scarborough

All rights reserved. No part of this publication may be
reproduced or transmitted in any form or by any means,
electronic or mechanical, including photocopy, recording
or any information storage and retrieval system, without
permission in writing from the JB Johnson Agency.

Requests for permission to make copies of any part of the
work should be mailed to the following address:

JB Johnson Agency
PO Box 1641 / El Campo, Texas 77437

Rattle Tattle ©
Published by Tadpole Press 4 Kids

ISBN: 978-1-933660-10-3
(HARDCOVER)

First Edition Hardcover
June 2007

Printed in China

Tadpole Press
...4 Kids.
A Publishing Division of Smooth Sailing Press

PO Box 1439 / Tomball, Texas 77377
SAN# 257-2680

This book is dedicated
to my grandparents, J. and Marie Bridges,
who have truly been a blessing in my life.

Telly Finkle was a young, plain, slender brown snake that lived in a deep, quiet hole under a smooth, flat gray rock. He was so plain that when he lay very still on his rock, basking in the sun, most of the animals passing by thought he was a brown stick.

Telly didn't have very many friends in the forest. One reason was because Telly smelled awful. He was so stinky that all the animals of the forest avoided him whenever possible. Even the skunks in the forest stayed away from Telly. He was often teased by the animals and was called names like Smelly Telly and Stinkle Finkle.

Telly knew that he was stinky. It was obvious how everyone avoided him, but as if that was not enough, Telly always had a cloud of flies that swarmed around his body and hung around his rock. He tried his best everyday to smell better, but it did not matter how often he wiggled in the blossoms of the pink and purple irises around his rock, he was still stinky. What Telly really needed was a good, long, soapy bath, but this was not an option because he was more afraid of water than anything.

None of the animals in the forest knew that Telly was afraid of water, but what everyone did know was that the main reason Telly could not keep a friend was because he loved to tattle.

Telly loved tattling more than anything else in the world. He spent all of his time sneaking and slithering ever so quietly through the tall grasses and irises hiding and listening to the conversations of the forest animals as they passed by his rock. This was the only time Telly was grateful that he was just a plain brown snake. No one ever knew he was there so he could listen for hours and hear things that were not meant for him to hear.

As soon as he heard a good secret being told, he would grab his favorite hat from under his rock and sneak out of his hiding place. Telly would and go to find his only true friend in the entire forest, a big old dark green bullfrog named Willard Warts. Telly tattled to Willard Warts every single day about all that he had heard.

Unlike Telly, Willard Warts had many friends. He was not very handsome because he had huge bulging warts covering his entire body. Willard Warts had very soft, caring eyes on which he wore the tiniest eyeglasses, and no matter what, rain or shine, he always had a smile on his face.

Willard Warts was one of the oldest creatures in the forest and was loved by everyone. He spent his time resting on the lily pads at the edge of the watering hole waiting for unsuspecting flies to get close enough that he could catch them on his sticky tongue with lazy effort.

Willard Wart's favorite lily pad was in the most beautiful part of the watering hole. Along one side, there was a majestic oak tree whose base and roots were covered with wild flowers and patches of soft grasses. Its large, heavy limbs covered with brightly colored green leaves hung low over the water, casting a large, cooling shadow. Willard Warts loved to watch the shadows of the leaves in the water as they danced in the breeze.

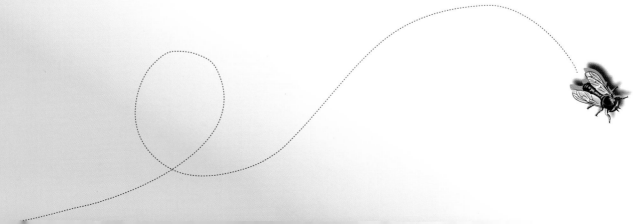

Willard Warts was very old and he never left the watering hole anymore. But he was never lonely as he had many thirsty visitors stop by for a quenching drink or a cool bath.

Willard especially looked forward to Telly's visits because there was always a large swarm of freshly buzzing flies around Telly. With a meal so enticing, Willard Warts did not care how bad Telly smelled. He would take a mouth full of plump, crunchy flies, stink and all, any day of the week!

Telly, on the other hand, hated the watering hole, since he was not a fan of bathing or water in general. Going to it was the only way he could tattle-tell to Willard. Telly knew that Willard Warts did not like him tattling to him because he had told him so on several occasions. Telly just could not help himself, so day after day, he found himself back at the watering hole eager as ever to tattle-tell his news.

One day, while Telly lounged around his rock, he heard Mr. and Mrs. Rooter and their twelve piglets approaching. All but one of the piglets looked exactly like Mr. Rooter – black with large white spots on their backs and bellies. The only girl looked just like Mrs. Rooter – solid red. Mr. Rooter always had his thick black hair combed straight back and every time Telly saw him, he had a fair amount of fresh dirt sitting like a decoration on top of his nose! Mrs. Rooter, always with a clean snout, wore a tightly woven necklace made of small white daisies under her double chin.

When Telly saw the Rooters coming, he quickly slithered out of sight into the tall grasses around his rock. He pulled his long, slender body up through the grass just high enough so that his head barely poked out and listened as closely as he could. What would he hear today that he could tattle to Willard Warts?

"Well, I told you she was getting too picky anyway!" said Mr. Rooter to Mrs. Rooter, as they approached Telly's rock. "If she doesn't want to get her snout dirty and dig up her own grubs, she can just go hungry! Why, when I was her age, I was already fending for myself... *My* papa didn't grub for me!"

Telly smiled with excitement at the conversation he was hearing between Mr. and Mrs. Rooter about their daughter. He wondered what was going to be said next. Was Mr. Rooter really going to let his daughter starve? Was he going to make her dig her own grubs from now on?

Oh, the suspense was eating Telly alive. Just about the time that he was sure he was going to hear the answer, a large drop of rain hit him square between the eyes. "Oh! NO!" thought Telly. He quickly retreated into his home deep under the rock.

Down under the cool rock, Telly could not hear their conversation. He could, however, hear the drops of rain beginning to come down very hard. He cringed at the thought of being out in the open in the rain. Telly tried to poke his head out of his hole so he could continue to hear, but he just couldn't. The rain was already dripping off his rock and beginning to form small puddles on the trail in front of his home. Telly caught a glimpse of the Rooters waddling off to their own home, with all the piglets scattering here and there, some pausing to wallow in the quickly forming puddles on the trail, and some pointing back in the direction of Telly's hole. He could not hear clearly, but Telly thought he heard something that sounded a lot like Stinkle Finkle.

"Humph!" said Telly to himself. He was angry that he didn't
get to hear the end of the conversation, but he felt like what he did
hear was pretty interesting anyway and he couldn't wait for the rain
to stop so he could tattle to Willard Warts. What would Willard
Warts think about Mr. Rooter letting his daughter starve? Telly
paced back and forth in his hole, checking often to see if the rain
had stopped.

It didn't take long for the shower to move on. Although Telly wore his best slicker and hat, he had to dodge the rain drops that were falling from the leaves on the trees while avoiding the puddles. As Telly approached the watering hole, he paid very close attention not to get too close to the water's edge.

Willard Warts was in his usual shady spot among the lily pads. As Telly approached, he saw that Willard was lazily staring in the direction of a perfect rainbow that had formed in the clearing of the forest. Telly noticed that his glasses were barely perched on the tip of his nose almost to the point of falling off.

Willard held in his hand a leaf just large enough to cover his head, keeping the occasional drops of rain from the big oak tree from hitting him on the head. Each time a drop hit the top of the leaf and rolled down onto Willard's back, Telly would shiver.

"Willard!" Hollered Telly, "You have to hear this!" Willard Warts opened his eyes with a startled jerk and in doing so his glasses fell completely off his nose onto his lily pad. He picked them up and placed them squarely on his round face and looked at Telly.

"Well, you don't need to yell at me, Sonny. I may be old, but my hearing is just fine. You should know better than to sneak up on an old bullfrog!" said Willard Warts. Eying the flies that were buzzing around Telly's head the old bullfrog said, "Why don't you come a little closer?" Telly cringed at the thought of getting too close to the water's edge, but he moved just a bit closer to Willard, sharing the bullfrog's leaf umbrella.

"Now son," said Willard Warts, "I've told you..." Willard's long sticky tongue shot out of his mouth mid-sentence and caught one of the unsuspecting flies, "time and time again how I feel..." Again Willard's tongue shot out of his mouth catching a fly, "about tattle-telling."

Telly got a bit tickled watching Willard Warts and trying to understand what he was saying while munching on a mouth full of flies.

 "Why do you continue to listen to everyone else's business and then tattle to me? Don't you understand how bad it is to talk about others? It can hurt your friends if what you are spreading around is nothing more than hearsay." Telly replied, "No one ever bothers to talk to me. I'm just plain, stinky Telly – nothing special. I guess that's why I like to tattle. It makes me feel important and at least everyone listens to me when I've got something interesting to tell."

"Well," said Willard Warts, "Being plain isn't so bad, you know. Your color makes it difficult to see you and that can keep you safe." Willard said quietly to himself where Telly couldn't hear, "Although, those flies are going to give you away every time!" Willard Warts continued, "You are also very small so you can hide in places that other animals can't. These are special talents that only you have, but if you do not appreciate them, they might be taken away or replaced with something you may not want. You have a great talent for bringing me dinner, too," laughed Willard Warts as he caught another fly.

Willard Warts crinkled his nose a bit, as Telly smelled very stinky and now that he was full, he began to regret asking Telly to get so close. Willard stood up, carefully lifting his wrinkled layers of skin and belly as he moved and slowly repositioned himself on a lily pad. He settled himself back down in a more comfortable position. With his belly now full of all the tasty flies, Willard simply wanted to return to his favorite spot and lazily ponder the now fading rainbow.

"Willard?" said Telly.

"Hmmm?" said Willard Warts quietly.

"Can I tell you a secret about myself?" asked Telly moving slightly closer to the edge of the watering hole and peered into the glassy surface.

"Sure," said Willard Warts, looking through his glasses over his wart-covered shoulder.

"I'm scared of the water," said Telly.

Willard Warts stopped crinkling his nose and smiled at Telly. "You and me both, kid," said Willard Warts.

Telly looked up at Willard Warts in surprise.

"Haven't you ever wondered why you never see me in the water? I'm always sitting on the lily pads close to the edge of the bank. I like to dangle my feet in, but I don't get into the water because I can't swim," said Willard Warts.

"I guess I never paid that close attention," said Telly.

"No, you were always so worried about tattling, you just didn't notice.

Telly smiled at him as he moved closer to where Willard Warts had settled.

"Thanks for telling me your secret, Willard," said Telly. "I promise I won't tell anyone."

"I'd appreciate that Telly," said Willard. "I just thought since you were telling me your secret, I'd go ahead and share mine, too."

Telly and Willard Warts now both looked toward the rainbow in silence.

"Telly?" Asked Willard, "Do you suppose that's why you always smell so stinky?"

"I suppose so," said Telly, "I have become used to it, although I don't much care for the flies."

"Well, I appreciate them," said Willard smiling, "but I am afraid that you may be missing out on making good friends because of this problem."

"I don't need more friends," said Telly, "I've got you!"

Willard Warts just smiled his best smile.

"I guess I'm going to head back home," said Telly.

"Okay." said Willard, pinching his nose, "See you later."

Telly turned to leave. "Oh, Telly," croaked Willard Warts, "Remember what I said about your special talents. There is nothing wrong with being plain or small. You don't need to tattle to be important."

Telly arrived back at his rock around dark. He was so proud of himself that he had actually made it all the way home without tattling to anyone, about anything. The special secret that Willard Warts could not swim weighed heavily on his mind. Willard Warts was his only true friend. Boy! Willard trusted him with a secret, but he, Telly Finkle, would be the center of attention with that news, no matter how stinky he was! "I must try to keep it to myself," he thought. "I made a promise!" These things and Willard's other comments about his special talents swam around in his thoughts as he fell asleep.

While Telly slept, he dreamed about Willard Warts and the special secret. In his dream, the forest was alive with activity. All of the animals were around the watering hole chattering and playing. Nobody even noticed that Telly Finkle was there. First, Telly tried clearing his throat to get their attention but no one even looked in his direction. Frustrated, Telly shouted, "Willard Warts can't swim!"

All of the animals just stopped and looked at Telly in shock.

Didn't you hear me, "I said, Willard Warts can't swim!" As soon as the words escaped his mouth the second time, there was a loud crack! Everything in the forest went silent. All the animals were watching in amazement as a large rattle on Telly Finkle's tiny tail appeared. Although this was a strange shock to Telly, it did not stop him from blabbing out again, "Willard Warts can't swim!" Again, a loud cracking noise was heard throughout the forest and still another rattle appeared next to the last rattle.

The animals stood still watching – unaffected by the news. Some, though watching, were still munching on the bits of grasses that hung out of their mouths. In desperation for some reaction from the animals other than blank stares at the growing rattles on his tail, Telly Finkle began shouting over and over, "Willard Warts can't swim! Willard Warts can't swim! Willard Warts can't swim!" Telly's shouts were echoed by a sharp...

Crack! Crack! Crack!

Three more large rattles had formed on the end of his tail! All of a sudden, Telly's tail began to shake vigorously back and forth! The rattles were so large and heavy that it shook Telly's entire body to the point that his eyes were swirling around and around in his head. With fear in their eyes, all of the animals ran away from Telly.

Even the flies flew away in terror! "Wait!" Telly's voice quivered, "It's just me, Telly, Telly Finkle!" But the animals didn't stop to listen to him; they just darted in every direction, trying to get away from the loud cracking of the rattles. Telly tried to stop the rattles from getting louder and louder, but the harder he tried, the louder they rattled.

Telly, alone and dizzy, lay down in the grass and began to cry. He was not the center of attention. He was completely alone. He did not feel important. He felt miserable. He had no way of hiding now. The rattles were unbearably loud and he certainly wouldn't have any friends for sure, especially not Willard Warts.

"Why did I tattle like that?" Telly cried to himself. "Why?" "Why?"

Knock! Knock! Telly looked up. He was still crying, but he was not in the forest clearing. He was under his rock. There was bright, morning sun shining into his hole. Telly looked down at his tail. It was plain and brown.

"It was just a dream!" Telly said to himself. At that moment, Telly heard a familiar voice. It was Willard Warts.

"Willard," questioned Telly. "Is that you?"

"Yes," replied Willard Warts, peaking down into Telly's hole.

Willard Warts was wearing a pair of pink and blue polka-dot shorts with bright yellow suspenders that pulled the waist of the shorts

up to his underarms.

The old bullfrog had a long stem of grass hanging loosely out of the corner of his wrinkled mouth.

"What are you doing?" asked Telly, "You have never left the watering hole, and what is that you are wearing?"

"I know," said Willard Warts, "I look ridiculous. These are my cousin Fred's swimming trunks. I borrowed them from him yesterday after you left. I just couldn't stop thinking about our conversation and I thought to myself that maybe you and I could work through our secret water problems together."

"What do you mean?" asked Telly.

"What I mean is this," said Willard Warts, "I'm not afraid of the water, I just don't know how to swim. You know how to swim, you're just afraid to get in the water. Why don't we help each other? That's what good friends do, don't they? What do you say, friend? Do you want to help out an old bullfrog?"

"Ok," said Telly, "What do you want me to do?"

As Telly and Willard made their way back to the watering hole, Willard Warts told Telly his plan for how they could help each other and Telly told Willard all about his dream.

"Are you upset with me, Willard?" asked Telly.

"No," said Willard, "You didn't really tell anyone, you just dreamed you did. Willard patted Telly on the back. Telly looked at Willard and smiled. He knew that he loved Willard more than he loved to tattle and he never wanted to feel like he did in his dream again.

Looking at the sparkling surface of the watering hole Willard placed a rose petal swimming cap on his round bumpy head. "Alright," said Willard, "I guess the first step is to get in! I'll be with you every step of the way, friend, and you will be with me. Ok?"

"Okay." said Telly.

It was at this moment that Telly noticed the long rope with a strange but fragrant object attached to it around Willard Wart's neck. Wondering what the object was, but without questioning, Telly Finkle took a long, deep breath and began to very slowly enter the water with Willard.

"This isn't so bad. Its actually pretty nice." said Telly smiling at Willard.

"Yeah it is." said Willard Warts, holding on tightly to Telly with his wrinkled flabby legs and toes sprawled afloat behind them.

"Do you think I will be able to make friends now that I'm not going to tattle anymore?"

"Sure," replied Willard Warts, "But it will take some time

for you to earn their trust again...and I think the fact that you are in the water is going to help tremendously as well."

"Oh really?" said Telly, "Why is that?"

"You'll see," said Willard Warts.

"What's that thing around your neck?" asked Telly, curiously eyeing the object on the rope now floating on the surface of the water between them.

"A bar of soap," Willard replied.

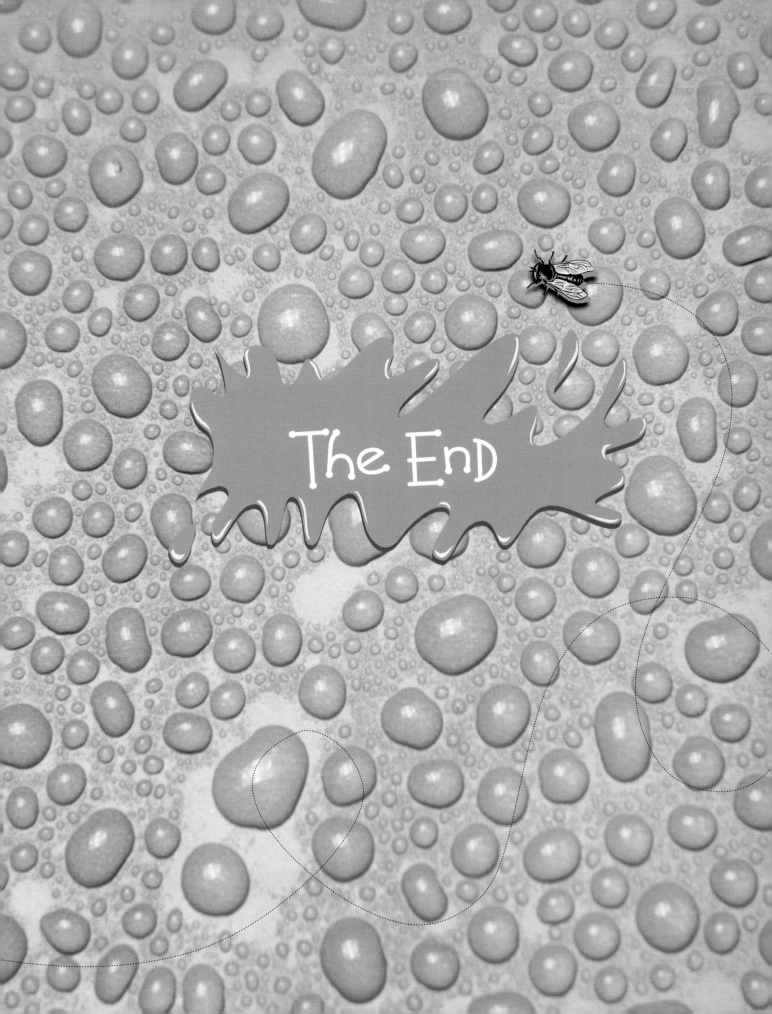

The End